Flowers from Mariko

by **RICK NOGUCHI & DENEEN JENKS**

illustrated by **MICHELLE REIKO KUMATA**

LEE & LOW BOOKS Inc.

New York

ACKNOWLEDGMENTS
The authors would like to give special thanks to Lloyd Inui and James
Gatewood for their advice on the historical accuracy of the story.
Inspiration for *Flowers from Mariko* came in part from the book *Nanka
Nikkei Voices: Resettlement Years 1945-1955,* published by the Japanese
American Historical Society of Southern California (1998).

The artist would like to acknowledge In The Beginning, a fabric store
in Seattle,Washington, which created many of the period fabric designs
featured in the illustrations.

Printed in Hong Kong by South China Printing Co. (1988) Ltd.

Book Design by Christy Hale
Book Production by The Kids at Our House

The text is set in Candida.
The illustrations are first rendered in ink and gouache resist to create
black and white drawings. The drawings are then scanned into a computer
and colored. Fabric and textured papers are also scanned and used to
create patterns in the illustrations.

10   9   8   7   6   5   4   3   2   1
First Edition

Library of Congress Cataloging-in-Publication Data
Noguchi, Rick.
Flowers from Mariko / written by Rick Noguchi & Deneen Jenks;
illustrated by Michelle Reiko Kumata.— 1st ed.
p. cm.
Summary: When she and her family are released from the Japanese American
internment camp where they have spent the last three years, Mariko plants
a garden to raise their spirits.
ISBN 1-58430-032-9
1. Japanese Americans—Evacuation and relocation, 1942-1945—Juvenile fiction.
[1. Japanese Americans—Evacuation and relocation, 1942-1945—Fiction.
2. Gardens—Fiction.] I. Jenks, Deneen. II. Kumata, Michelle Reiko, ill. III. Title.
PZ7.N67195 Fl 2001
[E]—dc21   2001029401

For our daughters, Miyako and Hana.
—R.N. & D.J.

For Mom and Roger, thank you for your love and support always.
For Dad, Agnes, Julie, Allie and Ben, thank you
for always being an important part of my life.
For my friends and family who encourage my creative spirit.
—M.R.K.

Mariko had been waiting almost
three years for this day, when she
and her family were finally allowed
to leave Camp. She scanned the
horizon all the way to the buttes,
but the saguaros were no longer
blooming. She'd always wanted
to explore the buttes, especially
in spring when the cactus flowers
blossomed, but no one in Camp
was allowed outside the barbed-
wire fence.

Mariko remembered the time nearly three years ago, shortly after Japan attacked Pearl Harbor, when she and her family, along with all the other families of Japanese ancestry she knew, were forced into Camp. The reasons were confusing to Mariko. "Just because I look like the enemy doesn't mean I am," she had told her mother angrily. "I am American. I was born right here in Los Angeles."

Mariko stood in the doorway and watched her father pull weeds from his garden. She thought about the gardening business he had left behind. She used to go along with him on his route and sing with him while they tended flower beds together. *Haru-ga kita. Spring is coming.* "Music makes the flowers grow," Father always said.

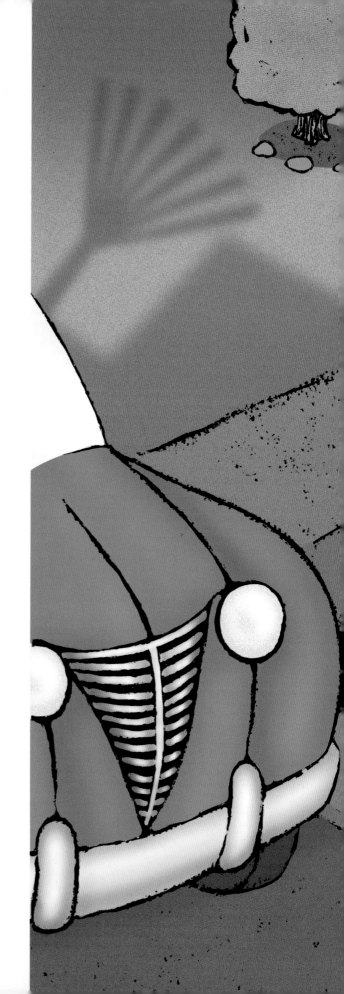

When they were sent to Camp, Mariko's father found it hard to leave his gardening truck behind.

"My business depends on it," he said sadly. But they were allowed to bring only what they could carry, so he was forced to leave the truck with their landlord, who promised to look after it.

Toward the end of the war, those who were willing to go East were allowed to leave first. Mariko was ready. She wanted to go back to a regular school and away from the desert heat and dust. But Mariko's father wanted to return home to California to start his business again. So they waited another year before the government finally let them leave.

The day Father left Camp to get his truck for the family's journey home, Mariko gave him a big hug. "Be careful," she said. While she was excited about going home, she had also heard rumors that people returning from Camp were not welcome.

A few days later, Mariko and her little sister Emi were outside playing marbles when they heard footsteps. They had expected Father to drive up in a cloud of dust. Instead he arrived on foot, his shoulders drooping, his glasses thick with dust. "My truck was gone," Father said. "The landlord sold it and now he's left town. No one knows where he went."

Maybe it was the saguaros towering behind him, their heavy arms raised toward the setting sun, that made Mariko's father look so small that day.

Instead of driving to California in their own truck, Mariko's family had to take the bus. As soon as the bus began moving, Mariko felt anxious. She didn't know whether she would ever see her friends from Camp again. She was also worried about making new friends. Mariko wished she could be like Emi, who was too young to remember life before Camp. All Emi cared about was finding an ice cream store when she got out.

During the long bus ride, Mariko and Emi fell asleep. Mariko woke just as the bus arrived at their temporary home, a trailer park built for those returning from Camp. Mother said the trailers were provided by the government for families who didn't have anywhere else to go. The dull silver trailers reminded Mariko of Camp. They were arranged in rows just as the barracks had been, with communal bathrooms in the center.

Weeks passed and Father could not find work. "Don't worry. We'll be fine," Mother told her. But Mariko knew her parents were worried. Through the thin walls of the trailer late at night, she could hear them whispering, their words circling the dark rooms like birds without a safe place to land.

Twilight soon became Mariko's favorite time. When the sky grew dark, she and Emi stood outside and waited eagerly for the bonfire. After the men gathered wood and started the fire, the glow from the flames lit up everyone's face, including her father's. When Mariko looked at him then, she almost felt as if everything were fine.

Mariko felt lonely in school. Most of the kids were not friendly and she didn't make any new friends. One day, on her way home from school, Mariko saw her father rummaging through trash barrels on the street. Embarrassed, she waited for her classmates to pass before approaching him.

"Hey, look at this!" her father said, pointing to a watering can, a shovel with a broken handle, and a lawn mower so old and rusty that Mariko almost didn't recognize what it was. "Here," he said, handing her two small envelopes he had also found. "I need to repair these tools. I don't have time for this."

Seeds. They were for the same kinds of flowers Father had planted in his tiny garden in Camp. Walking home, Mariko decided she would plant the seeds for Father. The flowers would cheer him up, she thought, remembering how everyone at Camp had smiled when they passed his flower garden.

Mariko looked at the packages, read the instructions, and studied the diagrams. Then she spent the rest of the afternoon loosening the ground in front of their trailer. By the time Mariko had finished planting and watering her seeds, her hands had blisters.

For the next several weeks, Mariko tended her plants faithfully. She also began singing to them, softly, as if she were passing along a secret. *Haru-ga kita. Spring is coming,* she sang as she watered and weeded her garden. Father walked by every day, but he never seemed to notice, not even when green shoots sprouted from the earth.

Mother knew Mariko was disappointed. "Just be patient, Mariko," she said. "Your flowers hear the music. Father will, too."

One day Father stopped when
he heard Mariko softly singing a
song to her plants. "I haven't heard
that tune for a long time," he said.
"You still remember." He took off
his glasses and wiped them with
his handkerchief, then smiled.
"Yes, spring is coming," he said.
For a moment, Mariko saw the
worry fade from his eyes with the
setting sun.

The first day Mariko's flowers
bloomed, she yelled happily for
her family. "Look, look!" she said,
pointing. "We have flowers!" Father,
Mother, and Emi sang with her,
their voices filling Mariko with a
glow as bright as a bonfire.

At dinner that night, Father made an announcement. "I'm going back into the gardening business," he said, beaming. "I finally got enough equipment fixed up to get started. And Mr. Johnson at the hardware store has already given me my first job."

"*Omedeto-gozaimasu!* Congratulations!" Mother said. "You did it."

"Yes, Father," said Mariko. "Congratulations!"

When the men built the bonfire that night, Mariko decorated herself with flowers from her garden, then skipped around the fire with Emi until they were both dizzy. When Father motioned for her, Mariko thought she was in trouble. Instead he took a flower from her hair and looped it through his buttonhole. "Your flowers are beautiful," he said, giving her a hug.

Everything was going to be fine, Mariko decided, as she watched her father dance across the trailer park, his shadow stretching taller and taller with each new step.

AUTHORS' NOTE

During World War II, soon after Japan attacked Pearl Harbor, President Franklin D. Roosevelt signed Executive Order 9066, which ultimately led to the forced removal of more than 120,000 Japanese Americans from their homes and businesses on the West Coast, interning them in concentration camps. The government referred to these camps as "relocation centers."

On December 17, 1944, almost three years later, Public Proclamation Number 21 was issued, rescinding the exclusion orders caused by Executive Order 9066. Japanese Americans were finally allowed to return to the West Coast. Most, however, no longer had homes or property to return to, and of those who did, many discovered that their possessions had been stolen, vandalized, or sold. Approximately 44,000 people remained in the Camps even after they were free to leave, simply because they had nowhere else to go. They were encouraged, then compelled, then finally forced to leave. Those who remained when the Camps closed were given $50 and put on a train or bus back to where they had been picked up.

The Resettlement years were a time of readjustment for most Japanese Americans. Though none of them were ever proven to be dangerous to the United States during World War II, many continued to face racial prejudice as they attempted to make new places for themselves and their families in the community.

More than 45 years after the forced incarceration of Japanese Americans, the United States government passed, and President Ronald Reagan signed, the Civil Liberties Act of 1988. This act acknowledged that the exclusion, forced removal, and mass internment of Japanese Americans during World War II were violations of their Constitutional rights. The act included an official apology.